Sailor Ted

Ship's Log

This book belongs to
Sailor Ted shipmate:

_____

_____

Welcome Aboard!

The Adventures of

SAILOR TED

& Shipmates

The Big Rescue

Sailor Ted, Captain of the Isle of Wight Car Ferry, and his first mate Charlie, were standing on the bridge gazing across the Solent to the Isle of Wight. It was their last crossing of the day.

The ferry was full of happy passengers looking forward to their summer holidays. All of a sudden a yacht called 'The Lady Solent' cut straight across the bows of the ferry!

"We're going to hit her!" shouted Charlie. Ted quickly spun the ship's wheel.

"PHEW! That was a near miss." said Ted, giving a loud blast on the ship's whistle.

'The Lady Solent' continued on its way as if nothing had happened.

"Is it safe to look now?" asked Charlie, taking his hands from his eyes.

"Who on earth could have been sailing like that? It was downright dangerous!"

Ted smiled. "Oh, I'd know that face anywhere! That was Disaster Dave – the worst sailor on the Isle of Wight!"

Ted guided the ferry into its mooring at Yarmouth. "I'm glad that crossing is over!" he said to Charlie. "I'm looking forward to a quiet afternoon - that was enough excitement for one day!"

Charlie nodded his head in agreement. "I'll go and make sure the cars unload safely."

The ferry's ramp was lowered and the eager passengers started the engines of their cars. Most of them had come to the Isle of Wight on holiday and were anxious to get to the beach as soon as they possibly could.

"Steady on!" said Charlie, " We don't want any accidents. One at a time please!"

Once Sailor Ted had checked that everyone had disembarked he left the ferry for the day. His dog, Ruby, was waiting for him on the quayside. "Come on Ruby," he said, "we're going to be busy this afternoon."

As they walked through the town everyone gave them a cheery wave. Mr Chops, the butcher, always made a fuss of Ruby and gave her a special treat. "I hear you are moving into your new house today Ted." he said.
"Yes," replied Ted, "I'm really looking forward to living in Yarmouth."

Ruby was looking forward to living in the town too. She would get a special treat from Mr Chops every day!

Sailor Ted was really happy as he looked out over the balcony of his new home. Ruby had curled up in her favourite chair in front of the window. She would be able to watch Sailor Ted's ferry going in and out of Yarmouth Harbour all day.

"The sea views from here are wonderful," said Ted. "Mr Brick has done a really good job of building our new house. I know we'll be really happy here Ruby." He rubbed Ruby's head and smiled as she wagged her tail in agreement.

They soon had Ted's favourite pictures hanging on the wall and the new house started to look just like home. Ted unpacked his telescope and put it to his eye. "Now let's have a look at what is going on out there." he said, as he swung his telescope along the horizon.

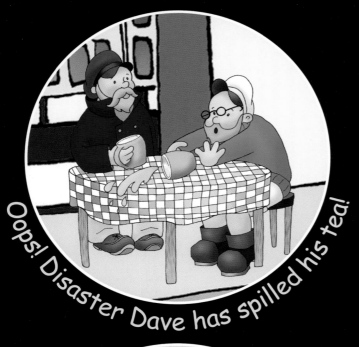

Oops! Disaster Dave has spilled his tea!

Ruby's sister Sienna has stolen some sausages!

The fisherman has caught an old boot!

The Inshore Lifeboat is ready for action!

Fergus the fishing boat is for sale!

The ferry is just leaving the harbour. GOSH!

There's Barney the open top bus on the quayside!

THAT IS A VERY LARGE OIL TANKER!

As Ted watched the oil tanker he could see that it was drifting towards the beach. "Oh goodness!" he said to Ruby, "That can't be right! The tanker is heading in the wrong direction. It looks as though it's out of control!"

Just then there was a loud 'whoosh' as the tanker sent up a distress flare. Sailor Ted knew they might not have much time as the tanker was in serious trouble. "Quick Ruby, we must telephone the rest of the inshore lifeboat crew and tell them there is an emergency."

Ted and Ruby rushed towards the quay, telephoning the lifeboat crew as they ran. There would certainly be a major disaster if they couldn't get to the tanker in time.

When Sailor Ted and Ruby arrived at the quay some of the lifeboat crew were already there struggling into their oilskins and sea boots.

Ted was really glad to see that his best friend, Old Tom, was among the crew. He would know what to do if it turned out to be a big rescue.

"I think we are going to need a tugboat for this rescue. What do you think Tom?" asked Ted.

"We will definitely need the tug for this job," answered Old Tom. "That's a very big tanker - too big for the inshore lifeboat to rescue on its own!"

The Coastguard Station at the Needles contacted Sailor Ted.
"Coast Guard to Sailor Ted! We have spoken to the captain of the tanker. He has lost all steering. If we don't act quickly he will run aground near the town - there could be a huge explosion!"

Ted looked out to sea again. The tanker was getting closer and he realised there may not be much time to spare!

"We will need to get the people out of the town to somewhere safe without wasting a minute. Come on Ruby let's hurry before it's too late!"

Ted asked the coastguard if Barney the open top bus was parked at the lookout point. The coast guard said it was.

"Right!" said Ted. "Ask the driver to come back down into Yarmouth as fast as he can. We will need him to get people out of the town and away from any danger!"

The coastguard rushed from the lookout tower and told the driver that Ted needed him urgently.

The bus driver jumped into the cab of his bus and started the engine. This is so exciting, he thought to himself, I have never done anything as important as this before!

"Full speed ahead!" he shouted as he raced down the cliff road back to the town.

Old Tom came steaming alongside in the tugboat.

"Listen to me shipmates." said Sailor Ted, "We are going to have to tow the tanker to safety. I will go in the tug with Tom. I will need three of the lifeboat crew to come with us." Some of the crew put their hands up to volunteer.

"That's good." said Ted. "The rest of you must go on the lifeboat and see if you can help to get the crew to safety."

Ruby jumped onto the tugboat with Ted. She didn't want to get left behind and miss all the excitement. There might be something I can do to help, she thought.

Ted got on the radio again, this time to the helicopter base at Lee-on-Solent.

The controller answered immediately, "Air Sea Rescue here." he said. "How can we help?"

"This is Sailor Ted. We are going to need the helicopter to air-lift the crew of a stricken tanker!" he told them. "It's drifting helplessly towards Yarmouth and if it hits the shore there is a danger it may blow up!"

The controller pressed the 'scramble' button and a siren sounded across the airfield. The pilot and crew realised there must be an emergency and ran as quickly as they could to their helicopter.

Back in Yarmouth, Barney the open top bus was racing around to collect as many people as possible. On the top deck with a loud hailer, PC Percival was instructing the townsfolk to leave their homes immediately. "Please hurry and board the bus." he called. "You might be in danger if you don't leave the town right away!"

The bus driver had never been this busy, rushing from place to place, picking up frightened people and taking them to safety. "Move along the bus," said PC Percival, "there is nothing to panic about. Sailor Ted and his shipmates are on their way to the tanker now to tow it away from the town!"

After a few hours the town was empty and PC Percival praised the bus driver. "Well done!" he said. "We couldn't have managed that without you!"

As the tugboat and the inshore lifeboat left the mouth of Yarmouth Harbour they could clearly see the tanker in the distance. "Full speed ahead!" shouted Sailor Ted.

The lifeboat crew opened up the throttle and the lifeboat sped forward, bouncing across the waves and sending up showers of spray.

The tugboat couldn't go as fast as the lifeboat but Old Tom made steady progress, ploughing through the waves towards the tanker.

In the distance they could faintly hear the engine of the Air Sea Rescue helicopter.

"It won't be long until we get there now." said Ted.

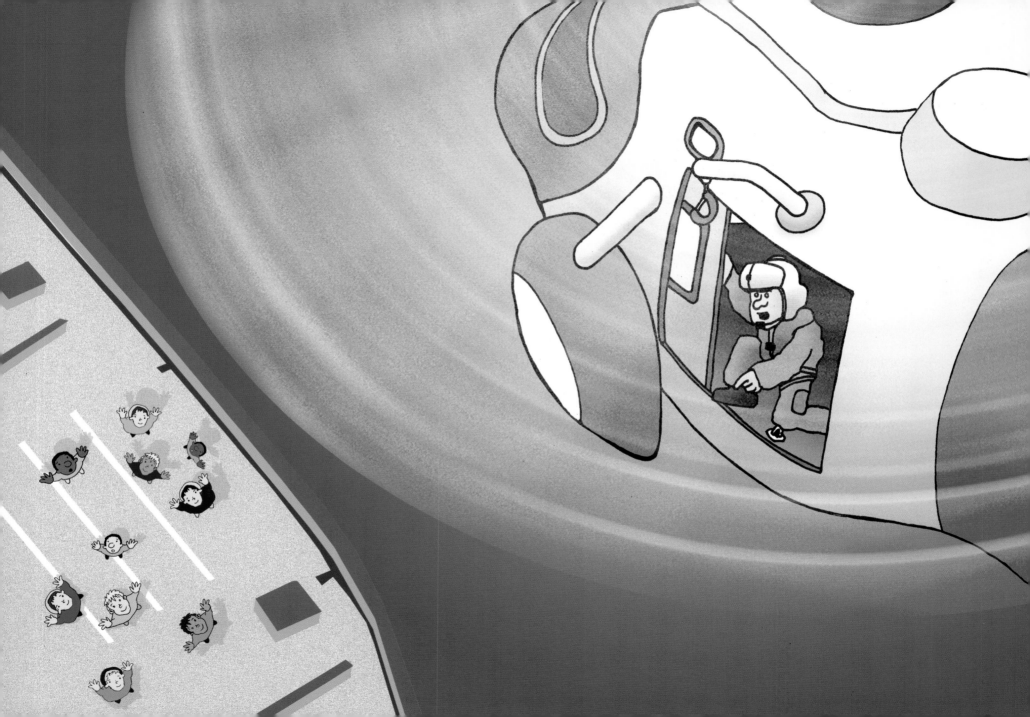

The helicopter pilot could see the tanker below him. The crew were jumping up and down on the deck waving their arms.

"Come in coastguard. This is the Air Sea Rescue helicopter," called the pilot into his radio. "We are above the tanker and can see the crew on deck. What are your instructions?"

"Reading you loud and clear Air Sea Rescue. Sailor Ted will be with you soon. When he gets there you can start to winch the tanker crew onto the tugboat. The inshore lifeboat will be standing by."

The helicopter did a circuit above the tanker. The pilot could see the two boats about half a mile away.

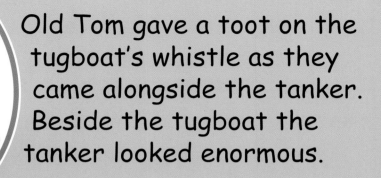

Old Tom gave a toot on the tugboat's whistle as they came alongside the tanker. Beside the tugboat the tanker looked enormous.

"This is going to be a tricky rescue." said Ted to the lifeboat crew. At that moment the helicopter pilot came on the radio.

"Pilot to Ted. Pilot to Ted." he called. "I'm just about to start winching the crew from the tanker. Will you be ready to transfer them to the tugboat as we don't have room for everyone on the helicopter?"

"Ted to Pilot. Don't worry - we'll be ready."

The sea was beginning to get rough and the tanker was heaving backwards and forwards with each wave that rolled into her side. Ted shouted to Old Tom to hold the tug as steady as he could. "Right you are Skipper." said Old Tom. "Steady as she goes!"

By now the tugboat was right up close to the tanker. "Prepare to start taking the tanker crew on board. The helicopter crew have begun winching them off so stand-by everyone!"

A few moments later the helicopter was hovering above the tugboat, ready to lower the first crewman onto the deck. "Right shipmates," shouted Ted above the noise of the helicopter, "Everyone in position? Let's get the crew off the tanker and away from danger as soon as possible."

Sailor Ted picked up his loud hailer and called to the captain of the tanker to throw him a line. It was time to tow his ship to safety.

Although he threw the rope as hard as he could, the tow-line was very heavy and fell short of the tug. The lifeboat crew groaned. This was going to make things difficult.

"We can't risk going closer to the tanker," Ted said, scratching his head. "If the boats bump together we might create a spark and cause an explosion."

Ted and the crew stared at the rope in the water wondering how to pick it up safely.

Ruby had been watching the rescue and wondering if there was anything she could do to help - she desperately wanted to be involved.

Then she saw her opportunity. In a flash she dived into the sea and swam towards the tow line. All the lifeboatmen cheered her on. The captain of the tanker waved his arms in encouragement.

Ruby swam bravely through the choppy seas until she got to the rope. Taking it between her teeth she turned and started the long swim back to the tug.

The rope was wet and heavy and it was as much as Ruby could do to keep afloat despite her life jacket, but she was determined. Eventually she got back alongside the tug.

As Ruby swam back alongside with the tow rope clenched between her teeth the crew let out a cheer. Ted leaned over the side and hoisted her from the sea. As soon as she was safely on board they all made a fuss of her and told her how brave she had been. "Well done Ruby." said Ted. He was really proud and gave her some dog biscuits as a treat.

"Secure the rope shipmates. Let's tow the tanker to safety." said Ted.

"Pilot to Ted." A voice came over the radio. Ted looked up and waved as the helicopter hovered above them. "Do you need any further assistance?" asked the pilot. "We have the situation under control thanks. Over and out." Ted replied.

"Back to base." said the pilot. "That's another job well done!"

Ted then radioed the oil refinery at Fawley.

"Fawley to Sailor Ted. We read you. How can we help?"
came the reply.

"We are towing a damaged tanker towards you." Ted told them.
"We need a safe berth to put her in."

"We were expecting you Ted. We have
prepared 'Berth 15'. You may take the tanker
straight in."

"Thankyou Fawley." responded Ted. "Just to be
on the safe side we may need a fire crew.
standing by."

"Understood! Fawley over and out."

As Sailor Ted and Old Tom steamed into Fawley they could see a fleet of fire engines assembling on the dockside.

"That must be our berth!" said Tom.

They brought the tanker to a gentle halt and dockhands immediately started to tie her up.

The tanker crew thanked Sailor Ted and his shipmates for rescuing them as they climbed from the tug.

"Well done shipmates," said Ted, "That was the biggest rescue we have ever done! Now full steam ahead back home to Yarmouth."

All the townsfolk of Yarmouth were cheering Sailor Ted and the lifeboat crew as they arrived back in the harbour. The Mayor was there to greet them. He made a speech thanking Ted and his crew for their bravery in saving the town from the drifting oil tanker.

The Mayor gave Ruby a big juicy bone as a reward for jumping into the sea and retrieving the towrope. He insisted they would not have been able to manage the rescue without her. Ruby wagged her tail and bounced up and down!

"We have laid on tea and cakes in the square." said the Mayor. "Everyone is invited!"

Sailor Ted and his shipmates led the crowd back into the square and all the townsfolk joined in the celebrations.

Sailor Ted and the lifeboat crew tucked into the tea and cakes provided by the Mayor.

Disaster Dave was at the next table, telling an old sea-dog the story of his latest mishap - a near miss with the Yarmouth Ferry!

One of the sea-dogs remarked that Disaster Dave had had more disasters than he'd had hot dinners and everyone laughed!

The chef from the harbour café shouted, "Three cheers for Sailor Ted and the lifeboat crew!"

"HIP HIP HOORAY!"

"HIP HIP HOORAY!"

"HIP HIP HOORAY!"

TED'S FAVOURITE PLACES & THINGS

The Solent

I WAS HERE!

I WAS HERE!

Newtown

I LIVE HERE!

I bough
postcard

Shalfleet

YARMOUTH

I WAS HERE!

FRESHWATER

Totland

Alum Bay

Isle

Yarmouth Lifeboat

Ted *Grandfather* SHORESIDE

TED19

Cha

Bla
C